Final Decision

Final Decision

FINAL DECISION: THE ENHANCED EDITION

Kala Holton

K&R

Acknowledge-
ments

Before April 2019 I had heard of suicide, of course who has not. I had come across people whose loved ones had committed suicide. I had people that I attended high school with that had committed suicide. But I had never had it impact me personally. I just want to say that suicide leaves those behind with so many questions and what ifs. We blame ourselves and wonder why we were not good enough for you to stay.

It does not matter what you have done, your life is precious too.

Thank you, Lord, for carrying me through those days. Thank you for my best friend Christy, my church family (Antioch Baptist of Sylvester), my loving children (all of you even the ones that I did not give birth to), my friends that had become family, my amazing co-workers and my extended family and especially my amazing husband Randy that never left my side I love you more than you will ever know. I could not have survived those first days, weeks, months, or even the holidays without you all by my side. I love each of you and will never forget your kind words or the fact that you were there for me in ways that I never knew I needed you to be.

Introduction

If you have been touched by suicide in any form, I will be honest this book may be tough to read, however, it will also show you how God uses things that seem impossible to turn for the greater good of your life. While some of the details of this book are completely from my imagination. This book is told from my experience of where suicide has touched my life in a hard and traumatic way. If you choose to read it, I pray that you find the healing through the experience of what life was like after my father committed suicide. While this story is fiction and not based on actual events. The feelings, emotions, and grace are very real.

While I am no expert by any means for the prevention of suicide or even for how to overcome the death of a loved one. I will tell you this God's grace is enough for all the above. It is what carried me beyond this earthly support and into his loving arms to get the message to you that you are enough, you are worthy, you are wonderfully and beautifully made.

I hope that this book helps you heal, and you feel the power of God in the mist of your tragedy. And if you are the one considering suicide because the devil has you convinced that you are not needed, loved or wanted. You are more than loved and more than wanted by so many that you have not even met yet. You are so needed by your family; they will be forever lost on this earth without you. Your friends will miss you more than you ever will realize. Seek help, seek medication, seek God first and foremost.

And please remember although these events seem like they are from real life experience they are not. Any mention or expression of such life events are simply stated as a coincidence. While I did experience my father committing

One

~

Chapter 1

"Daddy, Put it down."

"I'm sorry. I cannot, you do not understand, as much as I love you, I just cannot go on. I hurt all the time. Nothing is the same as it used to be, Karlyn. Everything is different than it was when I was twenty years younger.

"Dad, things change every day it is just life. That is no excuse to kill yourself. What is really going on dad? Have you done something that I do not know about? I mean talk to me dad, I cannot help you if I do not know what is going on?"

"Nothing, Karlyn. Nothing. I just cannot remember as easily as I once could. Now, I forget things. I give out to easily. I am tired Karlyn. I am tired."

"Dad, you are just depressed. It is normal and Dad there's help, I believe that you are experiencing depression Dad, there is help for this it is not a big deal. And we can get you help. You do not have to end things this way. Just lay the gun down dad. Do this for me if not for you."

My voice shaking with every word. I was scared. I did not want to see my father shoot and kill himself. There was no way out. No way to stop this from unfolding. I tried to sound strong. So that dad did not know how scared I was. I mean would he shoot me too. My mind flashed to a time before when I had seen this very gun pointed at me. I looked at Dad as a tear streamed down my face.

"Karlyn, I can't. I cannot. you do not understand."

I watched as dad paced with the gun in his hand. His steps more anxious than the previous.

"I am not going to jail. I love you girls."

"Dad!" I pleaded.

"Karlyn my decision is made. I made bad choices and I cannot change them. This is the only way."

"DADDY, NO!"

I watched dad's movements as he raised the gun up from his side. I watched as he looked at it. I see him sneak a look at me. I opened my mouth to say something to just keep him talking but no words came out. I sat silently with tears in my eyes as he turned the gun toward him. He placed the gun under his chin. Then he slowly raised the gun to his temple. Then he lowered it back to his chin.

"Daddy!" I whispered.

He looked at me.
He smiled.
And he pulled the trigger.

I closed my eyes as if doing this would help to block out the sound of the gunshot. I felt the blood as it splattered all over my face and shirt. I could smell gunpowder and fresh blood as it hung heavy in the air. The taste of my father's warm blood in my mouth as my scream fell on deaf ears.

Tears formed and streamed down my face at the realization of what had just unfolded in front of me. My body was shaking, my mind exploding, my heart broken.

The realization that my father had just killed himself washed over me as I sat in front of him and was helpless to stop him. I bent down and scooped up his lifeless body into my arms. I held him, as his body laid lifeless. I looked at his face, his greying hair, and bent to kiss his check one last time.

His face had stilled in an unrecognizable expression; forever silenced by his final decision. His body continued to lay lifeless as I held his head in my arms. The pool of blood beneath his head congealing on the floor and my jeans.

I am not sure how long I sat and begged him to

wake me from this dream. Begged him for just five more minutes. Minutes that would never come on this side of heaven.

"Daddy, NO!" I silently cried again. I thought if I begged him harder to wake up; if I continued to beg for this to be a dream that it would change my reality.

I was still holding daddy when the cops came in with guns drawn. I was covered in blood as I held daddy for the last time. My hero, gone forever.

"Daddy, we forgive you. We love you daddy." I whispered as I held his lifeless body holding his head in my arms as blood oozed from the gunshot wound and pooled at my arm, oozing over my legs, onto the floor. Congealing seconds later. I kissed him again on the forehead. This was my goodbye.

I felt the officer gently pull my arm and heard him say ma'am he is gone. Come with me so the medical examiner can do his job. I let him pull me away. I let him lead me to the road away from daddy's house. I allowed the officer to call my husband. I did not care that the news van was there. I did not care that there was neighbors and officers all there looking at me in disbelief. I did not care. My world was slowly crashing around me I felt like I was the one who was dying. I could no longer breathe on my own. I was just there; a fragment of who I had been just moments before. There were so many things that I wanted to say to him so many things that I wanted to tell him. And now it was too late it was too late to even say "Daddy, I love you too and I forgive you daddy."

The officer advised they needed to take my statement and that my clothing was needed for evidence. I was not sure what I was supposed to do but suddenly, as if an angel standing in waiting, my husband appeared and there in his hands was a change of clothes. I changed inside of the ambulance and allowed the paramedic to examine me to be sure that I was not harmed. I knew I was fine physically; Emotionally or even mentally I may never be fine again. Tears streamed down my face. I was not sure what would happen from here. It was obvious that dad killed himself but, there was always a chance that someone could believe that I had done it. After all it was my fault that I could not stop him. It was my fault that he was gone.

I had said goodbye forever to my hero, my daddy.

Two

~

Chapter 2

Present day

"Karlyn, Wake up. You are ok. You are safe. Wake up honey."

I slowly opened my eyes to see my husband hovering over me holding my hand, a worried look upon his face. As he gently attempted to awaken me so that he could console me from my dreams. Well really my nightmare. The same nightmare that I have had for the last several weeks now. Would I ever get this back under control? Would dad's suicide ever not be my fault?

"What's wrong I asked?"

"You were having the nightmare again the same one where you holler for your dad and you beg him to stop."

"I'm so sorry Scott, I did not mean to wake you."

"Karlyn, it's not a big deal that you woke me up but,

I am starting to worry about you."

"Scott, I am fine. It will pass. They say something like this takes months to recover from."

"Karlyn, I know it will take a while for you to

overcome this. But it has been a couple of months now. I am starting to worry as these dreams become more frequent. You seem more distant now then you were right after. I am just worried about you spiraling into a path of self-destruction or suicide yourself."

"Scott, I just have stuff to sort out that's all. I will not be planning to commit suicide or even making some self-destruction plans."

"You know your father's suicide isn't your fault right."

"Oh Scott, I know!" I let out a sigh of irritation. "Scott. But I still blame myself for not seeing the signs, for not being there to stop him. For not listening to my gut, for not standing up to him and fighting with him because I knew Scott I knew and instead of fighting I just walked away that day. I allowed him the opportunity to end his life. I did nothing. So, when you say it is not my fault. Scott, it really is my fault. It is my fault that I was not strong enough to stand there and tell him the truth after all these years. It was my fault for knowing and walking away. He would still be here if I had just taken the guns in the house."

I tried hard to hold back the tears as they begin to fall down my face. I could not control the shaking or the emotions anymore; they consumed me. I was desperate for answers. I was desperate for the pain and hurt to go away. I never understood why people wanted to take their own lives. What about those of us left behind to clean up afterwards. I could not just turn these emotions off. Obviously, dad felt so alone, like there was nothing for him here on earth anymore. I did not matter. My sister did not matter. The grandchildren did not matter. Nothing seemed to matter to him.

"I know you blame yourself Karlyn, but you have to believe me there is nothing you could have done to stop or prevent your dad's suicide."

"I did not get to say goodbye." I felt the tear slide down my face as my husband gently wiped it away as he had done many times before since that fate changing afternoon. The afternoon that took my children's innocence to this hateful world.

"Honey, I promise this will get easier with time."

"I do not know Scott. This pain, the guilt, the regret, it is almost too much to bear."

"Honey, you can do this. You can overcome this. You are not to blame."

"Mentally I know that. In my heart and soul though is another story. With every beat of my heart, I feel guilty. With every breath I take I feel the guilty."

"If you continue to blame yourself, Karlyn you too will follow in his steps."

With that sentence Scott walked out.

Three

∽

Chapter 3

Chapter 3

One month earlier

"Karlyn, we need to talk when you get a minute."'

"What's up Chenille?"

"Karlyn, no you better call me we cannot chat about this over a text?"

"Give me five Chenille."

Chenille was always involved in some type of drama. So, having her text and tell me she needed to talk to me was not surprising I was simply curious what she had going on this time. I finished up what I was working on and gave my sister a call. It had been a bit since I talked to her which was nothing new. We went for months at a time without talking it was our normal.

"Hey sis what's up?"

"Karlyn, we have huge problems?"
"Nah girl I am really good. But what is going on with you."

"Girl, someone just named our dad as their abuser."

"Do what?" I felt my heart quicken. My palms grow sweaty.

"Yeah, girl, he won't answer my calls. Will you try and get ahold of him make sure he is okay?"

"Yeah, I am on it. Do you know who it was?"

"Yeah, I really do but, I do not think you are ready to hear that part."

I started to ask Chenille more questions but realized that she had already hung up the phone. As I contemplated my next move, I realized that I really needed to call dad. He needed to hear it from me before anyone else. If I was honest with myself, I was not surprised for years I waited for the next time to come. Now that it was here, I was not sure I could handle this. I knew that dad would kill himself with this news. I could see it slowly unfolding. I shook the vison away as if it would change my gut feeling. I knew if it were true, he would never admit it, nor would he ever allow himself to go to jail. I could not answer how I knew but I had this sense of knowledge.

I knew that meant that Chenille knew this person personally and this could not be good news. None of the people Chenille hung around were good news so this was not a surprise. I still felt my heart rate increase. I still felt the impact of her words as they replayed in my mind. I did the only thing I knew to do and that was call my dad. I knew he was not perfect, and all these emotions flooded into me like I could not breathe. I could not handle this part of the news. Memories long buried flooded my mind. Memories that I wanted to stay buried.

I called dad. Because I knew that he needed someone to stand beside him. And that someone was going to be me this time around. I was not sure why I felt obligated to stand by his side. Was it for show? Was it so that my kids' image of the man not become shattered? The realization that I would protect my children at all costs hit me like a ton of bricks. I picked up the phone and called Dad.

"Hey dad it's me. What are you doing?"

Dad sounded as if he had been taking a nap when I called. I finally told him why I was calling so early in the day. I knew dad realized it was unusual as I usually talked with him only after work unless he called me during the day.

"Karlyn, are you okay? You do not usually call me this early in the day."

"No, Dad. It is bad news. Chenille said that someone has told that you have abused them and well I need to know dad is this true. And if not why would whoever this is said it? How does this person even know you? I do not understand dad. Can you shed any light on any of this?"

I waited for dad to respond and the other side of the line was quiet.

"Dad, are you still there?"

I listened to dads' words as he told me no it was not true. I listened to dad's words as he said he had no idea why they would say such a thing, His voice steady but not strong. My brain heard the words that were coming out of his mouth. But my heart seemed to be telling me something different. I was not sure what to listen to my head or my heart. I was shattered, heartbroken I felt helpless and utter despair. This was a conversation I never wanted to have with my father. I thought we had buried this years ago. And yet, here we were, Decades later in the same situation yet so different. Because this time the unbeliever was me.

"Alright dad, well I am still at work so I have to go but, I will check on you again in a little while."

I listened as dad hung up his end of the phone. I sat silent on the concrete steps of the office as I debated what Chenille had told me, and what memories flooded over me as I recalled a time of long ago back when I was just a young teenager.

I could not face this right now. I was in the middle of some serious stuff right now trying to prove that I was perfectly capable of handling college, a full-time job, and raising my teenage children all while taking on more children because they needed someone to call their own. Life was not fair that much was for certain.

I did not understand the holdup of the state telling me that I just did not seem qualified or capable with my busy lifestyle. The last thing that I needed was this to come to surface after all these years. I did not want that for my children. I did not want that for my husband. Who was I kidding I did not want that for me? The past deserved to stay there in the past.

I sat with my head down for a few moments until I had gathered my thoughts and walked back into my office. My heart was heavy. My fear was real. I was not sure what to expect over the next few days but, I knew that in the end my father would never stand trial for anything that he was accused of. I knew in the end this would be the cause of his death. I knew that I would have to say goodbye to my father.

I called Chenille back and told her that I had talked with him and that he was alright. I listened to her as she relayed the story of how everything had come to pass.

It was through her story that I realized that the

person she was speaking of was indeed remarkably close to her. I realized that the person in which she was protecting was her child. I was not sure what to think.

I knew that her child had a history of lying but I also knew at the same time what this man had done in his past. But could I let his past define who he was twenty years later. Or should I give him the benefit of doubt. I was not sure what to believe but, I knew that things were not going to just go away this time as they had done for me several years before. No one seemed to care back then. I had heard all the stories and new that it had happened to more than one child. I had heard all of this after I told my story. And well now it was too late. And this was the last thing that I really wanted to happen was for any of this to come to light. I had so many reasons of hiding these fine details of my previous life. Surely no one could touch the information from my childhood years, Right? There were laws on that stuff right. This was stuff that people could not pull up again after you became an adult. Right? Good gracious I sure hope so.

I tried dad several more times that day to reach dad. He did not answer; no matter how many times I called.

My throat automatically closed.

Tears filled my eyes.

I could not breathe.

I just knew deep down that daddy was gone. I did not want to be right. Why? Why God? Did I have to be right?

I felt convicted that this was the day that I was going to lose my dad.

I left and went to his home. Outside things were silent. I could not hear anything. I listened as I got out of the car. My heart raced. I could hear my heart beating in my ears. My breathing was fast and shallow. I walked inside of the gate, shutting it behind me. I could see the back door was open. Just the screen door. I peered inside scared of what I would find if I glanced inside of the glass.

Deep breathing I knocked on the door. I watched as Tank came to the door. His tail happily wagging. I awaited and there he stood as he opened the glass screen door to let me in.

He continued at the stove cooking eggs and sausage for him and his dog.

So many emotions went through me at this time.

My heart was relieved, my mind racing. I asked why he was ignoring my calls. I asked what was going on with him? We talked briefly and then I addressed the elephant in the room. I asked dad were the accusations true.

I will never forget his words.

I will never forget the look on his face.

I will never forget when he looked at me and his voice shook with his answer.

"I have no idea Kailyn where she got such a story."

The denial in his voice.

The answer that one always gets when they ask a person a hard question.

My heart fell; because I knew without a doubt looking at him that my father, my dad, my hero had just lied to my face.

I thought for a long moment as I considered my next question. I was not sure how he would answer or if he would be honest. I only knew that I had to ask, what would happen if I did not, and he did go through with killing himself? But what would happen if I asked, and he then decided to kill himself? I could not believe I was in this position.

I looked at dad for a long moment as his back was to me. When he turned around, I looked up and into his face. I asked him the question I dreaded the answer to.

"Daddy, are you planning to kill yourself?"
He looked at me without emotion on his face.

And with strong assurance he said no. I was then the stupidest person that I could have ever been, I believed him. I believed that this would go away. I believed that this would just be slide under the rug as it had been several years ago. I left him with promises to call later. I checked on him daily. And when I was not checking on him,

I was begging God to do something anything, because I did not want to deal with this situation in any shape or form. I would accept however God planned to resolve it.

I sat and just begged God to come and intervene to show me what to do. To show me what to accept and what to let go. I had so much going on in my life that I just did not want to be dragged into my sister's mess. I mean I had put my past behind me. I was not that person anymore regardless of how much my mother attempted to tear me down. I was still so much stronger and so much more than she ever gave me credit for. The pain that there was something that I could not put into words. I for once had no one that I could call and talk to about what I was feeling was extremely heartbreaking. You see my secret was supposed to die with me not be brought to light because of someone's inability to be a parent.

I was contacted seven days after Chenille called to tell me the things that were going on at her home. I told the woman who contacted me in no uncertain terms this was her problem to prove I would not help her. Her words floored me and would be words I would never forget.

"Your mother and sister said that you could help me make this case."

I sat and listened to the words replay in my head.

These two women that had turned their backs on me so many years ago expected me to help them now. Where were they then, where were they when I was this child. When they spat in my face and called me a tramp a liar. When they skipped my birthday not once but twice when I was nothing to them. They now expected me to just jump to help them to give up everything for them. There was no chance I was going to help them do anything, it was not that I was angry or revengeful, it was that I had buried those demons many moons ago. I was not in denial of the things of my past. That much was for sure. I had done what a born-again person does.

I had allowed God to heal me in ways that no therapist would ever be able to. I was not opening something that I had laid at God's feet on a beautiful Sunday and promised that it was God's I was not taking it all back now. Not now or ever. This was God's fight not mine. And I would remain neutral in this situation. I would stand firm on my faith.

It was in this moment that I knew Satan wanted me to take back the hurt and anger that I had laid at Jesus's feet. Because if I was suffering through moments of my past again, I was more likely to turn to evil things than if I remained kneeled at Jesus's feet. Praying his blood over me, his peace, and most importantly his love. It was by the Grace of Jesus I was healed from the past trauma. And by the Grace of Jesus, I could stand firm in my faith that he would and could walk me through whatever I faced. I trusted God to handle things. But I knew that somewhere along the way I too would suffer immense pain that I would not be able to put into words. Unlike others though, God would see me through this because I was His child. And His child alone.

It was that moment that I knew that this would be a hard few week. It was that moment that I knew no matter how much I tried to ignore this situation that it was not just going to go away.

I was tired of fighting; I was tired of fighting a woman that I called mom. I was tired of having to prove myself worthy of her approval, attention or love. I was past the point of feeling the need to prove who I was, of who I had become.

So, I prayed even harder. I prayed for God to intervene in ways that seemed impossible moments before. I prayed for God to do what must be done that would give Him the praise and the glory. I prayed most of all for His will to be done.

"Officer, I apologize that you were misinformed but, there is not any information I can give you."

"Just come in and talk with me."

"No, ma'am unless you have a subpoena for me, I will not be talking with you at all. Have a good day officer."

I disconnected the call. While I was nice and professional or so I thought I was also angry. Angry that these two people had tried their best to drag me into something that I wanted no part of. I almost hated them all over again.

I half expected a fight from her.

I half expected her to tell me I had no choice.

I half expected so many things but, what happened next was not what I expected.

It was not what I prepared myself for.

Four

~

Chapter 4

Mom called. She never called; you see she was the type of person that felt like everyone should call her. But where I come from both phones have the capacity to ring. To prove that point it was ringing now; proving me correct. That it too would ring upon someone calling.

The phone is not the only thing we do not agree on and maybe that is where I should just learn that maybe just maybe we do not even live on the same planet. To live and disagree. Was that even possible?

When she called this time though it was not a conversation I planned to be having. Long gone were the attributes that I would sit and listen to her as she nagged her way into my brain of how useless of a daughter I really was. Long gone were the days that I would cry because her words slashed through my skin to a deep burning scar. Long gone was the old me.

She wanted to talk about that year that she turned around and walked away from me. She wanted to discuss how wrong she was and what a bad thing she had just let unfold.

Whoa! Wait! She wanted to apologize. I knew I could not have heard her correctly. She never apologizes for things that are her fault. You see her and dad had that much in common.

Over twenty years, I waited to hear these words and realized that after twenty- five years I did not need to hear them after all.

It was in that moment that I realized that God had really healed my hate for the past. God had healed me on such deeper levels of forgiveness that I had not comprehended until that moment. I knew I was healed but knowing knowing was completely different than knowing.

The more she continued to speak the more I realized that God had led me here to realize my calling as well. This, this was not about me. This new developed situation between my sister and father; was not about me. I only had to watch this from the sidelines. God was using this to show me that I had grown. God showed me my calling and where I needed to be.

I was in this place because I was not supposed to adopt a single child or even a sibling group. Oh, I wanted to bring children into a loving family. However, I was to follow Christ. I was to be a mother to all the orphaned children across the earth. I was supposed to be sure that orphaned children knew that their story was not to stop inside that orphanage. That God had a plan for each of them.

I was supposed to be His voice to all his orphaned children that felt like they were forgotten. Oh but, I was sure my mother would have something to say about that as well. I was tired. Tired of everything when it came down to her. This would be the last time I ever had any intention of talking to her.

It was that moment that I knew I was done. I was tired of fighting a woman that seemed to want to destroy me.

It was that moment that I knew that this woman only cared about herself and how she looked to others.

I listened as she spoke and realized that if this were the last time, I spoke with her I would be okay with that. Did I genuinely believe that I would be okay with it or was I kidding myself? Was I sure that I could continue my life ignoring the fact that she still walked among us; alive and breathing much unlike my father that laid in a morgue somewhere?

The toxicity of this relationship ate at me emotionally, spiritually, and even physically. I could not keep up with this and maintain my sanity. But could I walk away? That question haunted me.

Days went by and slowly. Those days turned into weeks. I heard not a word from the officer or my mother again. Silence from my sibling as well. I talked to dad often. Until one day. My vision became a reality.

A real-life nightmare unfolded.

My father made the news.

He took his own life before being arrested.

People claimed he must have been guilty.

The comments of those that lived in the same town were awful. The words stung as they called him names. True or not those words carved a piece of me away.

The people and their hatred were awful. Would they see me the same way? Would I too be shunned? Would my husband love me if he found out the truth? What about my children? They, they could never know. These outsiders they did not understand. Regardless of what he had been accused of doing; Regardless of how they felt.

He was still a person.
He was still someone's father.
He was still someone's spouse.
He was still my father.
He was still my husband's father -n- law.
He was still my children's grandfather.
He was still my children's children great-grandfather.

And this is where my life fell apart.

I did not know how to handle this. I did not think that I could handle this. I was not sure I could carry on. And I had no idea how I ever would carry on.

I wanted my dad. Even if it where for five more minutes.

It appears that once someone is gone you can think of a million things that you should have said. Should have done. Things that you would never get the chance to do or undo.

When you find out from the news that your father is dead. It does something to you. It changes you in ways that words cannot describe. Maybe it is the way that you find out. Maybe it is just the fact that they are forever gone.

Maybe it could be the fact that you will never hear their voice, their laugh, or see their face again.

Regardless of what happens after that nothing seems to really matter anymore.

I got in the car and I drove. I drove with no destination in mind. I drove without seeing things pass me by.

I went to the scene I knew what I was going to find. I had seen the news story. I knew in my gut what I would see upon arrival after all the vision had made that noticeably clear. But surely anyone could tell me it was wrong. That all of it was just a big mistake. The vision, the news article, I mean news people get the story wrong all the time, right? Visions only happened during Biblical times, right? So, what I thought I had seen in what I called a vision was just simply my imagination. Right?

I pulled on to the street and what stared back at me was unreal. It looked like a movie set with sheriff cars, news vans, spectators standing outside their doors. Watching, Waiting. I sat for seconds although those seconds felt like minutes. I pulled through the series of cars, and trucks.

The scene set before me etched forever into my memory. A scene that I watched on television thousands of times yet, one that this afternoon I had much rather forget.

I watched the sheriff cars with their flashing lights and the police officers stand around talking about God only knew what.

The news anchor standing speaking into her microphone. Reporting only God knew what. I mean what more could she say. She had already released things that no daughter should ever find out online. I wanted to scream then and there.

I wanted someone to pay me some attention.

I wanted someone to pay.......

I opened the door before my mind could catch up with my what my body was doing. I got out of the car and with more confidence than I felt. I headed to my father's property.

There stood a young gentleman in uniform, who I was determined to get answers from.

"Ma'am you cannot be here." He stopped me as I walked toward the scene.

"Uhm yes sir I can and will. You see this is my father's and I demand to know what is going on."

My voice giving away the shakiness that I felt all over my body. I already knew. But I needed someone to verbally tell me what was going on. My gut knew but my heart and brain needed verbal confirmation.

"Ma'am step over here? I believe it is safe to assume that you would want out of the view of the camera."

Without hesitation I followed him I sure did not want my back side to be flashed all over the news stations. For the entire world to see.

I looked up at him. Looking into his dark brown eyes. I matched his gaze with one of my own. I know he felt me pleading with him; pleading him to tell me what I already knew was wrong.

I know when he looked at me in my eyes that he seen them pleading with him to tell me that my father was alive and just being arrested.

When did he not open his mouth, I quietly asked the question I dreaded the answer to; "Is my daddy still alive?"

He paused before answering. Debating on rather to inform me of the truth or tell me he did not know to buy some time and grab another officer.

He lowered his head. Pausing again to say. "No, ma'am your father is deceased."

His answer crushed my little heart. I felt like a child again. Learning that I could no longer have my favorite toy to sleep with. I searched his face for answers to questions that remain unspoken.

I felt my legs buckle... I felt him grab my arm and slowly lower me to the ground away from the cameras. Away from the onlookers.

I gathered my senses and knew that I had to

call someone. Anyone. I knew that I could not do this alone. I knew that I had been right all along, and she, she killed my father. I silently blamed her with everything I was. Ridiculous I knew however, I needed someone to take the blame. The should have's the should of all came flooding to me at once. Things that could no longer be done or undone the results stood confirmed in all of eternity. Daddy was dead. He had pulled the trigger himself. He had ended his own life. And I had to manage to clean up after him. But how? How could I do just that when I just wanted to lay in the road and wish this all away.

And I knew that from this point forward I was going to need God to carry me through every day. Through the long days and long nights. Through the decisions that would undoubtfully start coming. The skeletons that hung in the closet would soon be brought out to air. The secrets of a past so hidden that even I was not sure I could find it.

"God, this isn't the answer I expected. What are you doing? This, This, this cannot be your will.

This is not the answer I needed.

This is not the answer I wanted; you know that.

This is not anything I had hoped for in a resolution. Lord, what are you doing?

Why are you doing this to me? Lord why are you abandoning me?

Why? Lord, what will I do with daddy gone?

Why are you forsaken me when I need you more than ever?

I do not want to do this. God take time away. Rewind time. Let me just go back."

Five

~

Chapter 5

I sat on the graded road looking at everything yet seeing nothing. I knew that I had to call my husband I had to tell him something. I looked back at my car where my phone rested in the cup holder. It was then that I caught her standing in the street. She was watching, waiting, I felt threatened and before I could realize what I was doing I began screaming. I hollered like a banshee amid a jungle, I wanted her gone, I wanted her away from here. I wanted her.... Dead.

I pointed in her direction as I continued to scream at the officer to remove her from the area. He followed my finger to the woman standing in the road.

I treated her like a stranger. She was a woman that I knew yet I knew nothing about. She may have been the woman that I shared parents with. However, to claim her would be an embarrassment. She was not my sibling. She had lost me so many years ago. This choice left me alone.

I shared blood with this woman. Our DNA matched but that was all.

Realizing who I meant and what the angry scream indicated; another officer ran over to her. What are you doing protecting her? She does not need protecting she needs a bullet. A bullet between her eyes. I glared over to the officer that stood beside her. I was not sure what he was thinking about me at this giving moment. After all I was sure this scene was not one played out very often. The officer closer to me moved even closer to me. He lightly touched my arm. I glared at her one last time. And I looked at the officer that held my elbow.

I let him lead me to the side of my car. As the other officer led my sister to the end of the street in the opposite direction.

And people sometimes called officers stupid. Looked smart to me.

At least in this case.

I watched as they continued to lead her away.

They just avoided the confrontation of a lifetime. I was more than ready to eliminate her from this world. The anger I felt was real and powerful the hatred more than I could explain into words.

Was it possible to hate someone this passionately?

Would I ever forgive her?

Would I ever stop blaming her and her daughter?

Was it even really their fault?

I needed to call someone, I needed something... I slowly called my husband and begged him to come to me.

My earthly rock.

My real-life knight in shining armor.

Scott was already in route.

I did not really know what to do with myself.

Did I stay or did I go?
How would it look if I stayed?

How would it look if I left?

Would I seem like the uncaring daughter to go home?

How would someone that did not know me view me?

I wanted to scream again. I was so mad with God.

Why did He do this? I was not good enough....

I wanted to stay at the site but, what good was it really.

I did not want to be captured on camera.

I did not have anything to say to anyone. I just wanted to crawl into a dark hole.

I was angry.

I knew that angry words would do me no good.

No one could answer why or how had this happened?

I did not want to be here, but I did not want to leave either.

What if they needed me?

Could I see him if I stayed?

Could I look at him one last time?

I was officially the next of kin as my father was not married and I was his oldest child.

Next of Kin I had never had that label before.

I believed that I should have been notified like a standard next of kin. I mean the movies show that family gets a visit from an officer. And well since there were so many there, my thoughts were some-one could have at least phoned.

Six

~

Chapter 6

Local news.
Someone had to call them.
They just did not show up out of the blue.

Vultures. That is what they were. Vultures. Chasing, watching, twisting the story. Truth. They did not know the truth. They did not know the pain that went with the truth.

I was angry. I was angry on so many levels. The news, the sister, the situation. The list was long. Things that I was angry at.

I was angry that I had to learn of his death from the news.

Was I angry at my sister because she did not call me? Was I angry at the events that unfolded? Was I angry at myself for standing by and letting things land where they may?

I glared at the news van and just wished I could turn back time. I was not sure what I would do with a few hours of time before this happened. Would he have answered the phone if I had called him sooner today?

When things of this nature happen; You see my

biggest regret in this moment is that I did not talk to him yet today. I had failed as a daughter, I had not had the chance to tell daddy not to do this, tell daddy to listen to reason, tell daddy death was not the answer.

Remind daddy of his dog that he loved but did not cherish as he did his first dog. Haggy was his favorite and would forever be. She was laid to rest out back. I looked out at the house. I knew Tank was somewhere I just had to figure out where he was. I knew I had to take my fathers' dog home with me, I did not really want to. I was not sure what I was going to do with him. But I knew he was going home with me and we would do the best we could with him. I had given daddy the dog almost a year ago. I knew the dog knew me and I knew that somehow, I was expected to take care of him. This was confirmed for me in the many note's dad wrote me about little things that I found much much later.

However, little did I know what a chore that would be for me as I increased my family of dogs.

I asked the officer to show me dad's dog. They called for him, he did not come running. I was scared someone had snatched him even with officers standing all around. I called for him and out of the trees he ran wide open straight to me. He was a happy joker. And I wish I could have felt his enthusiasm and happiness as my heart was still breaking. I was not sure what I was supposed to feel like, but I did know that I felt more alone than I ever had before.

I decided that it was time to take Tank the dog to his home with me. I told Tank to load up in my car. All that dog hair was going to drive me insane if I was not already headed there. While I was getting ready to leave, I noticed that the bus was leaving the end of the road. I assumed that is where my sibling had disappeared to. I could see them as Chenille told her of her grandfather's death. I watched as his unnamed victim cried in the street because of his death. So dramatic. I was still angry. She could tell her kid in person, I found out from a news story that was released.

I drove to the end of the street where they sat. I let down the window and laughed at the scene before me. I reminded them they started this and that I had told them this is how it would be resolved. The hatred in my voice evident.

They began to scream at me. It was more than I could take. I was already on edge. I was over my limit. I could not handle anything more. I knew that I would not break but I could not promise taking a turn down a dark path that had no return.

I looked over at the loaded gun beside me, the temptation to end their lives strong. An eye for an eye, right? Do to others as they do to you? Isn't that what my mother had taught me all my life? It would be such a quick and easy death for them. Almost too good of a death for the people that had destroyed my life. This was not just about daddy committing suicide this was about so so much more.

This was about the lifestyle she chooses. This was about the times that I had been there for her. This was about being taken advantage of. This was about being used. The fact of how useless she was as an American Citizen sponging off the government never contributing but expecting a handout. I mean why was God keeping them here. They were just useless to society or the kingdom.

My faith in God was in question. Not at just why she was still walking the earth and daddy gone. Just gone in a quick second. There was no chance to say goodbye. Why would God do that? I had never thought of this question before when I heard of someone dying from a car accident. However, when it affected you there were things that you thought of that you have never thought of before.

Where was God in the mist of this?

The devil whispering in my ear. The devil telling me that they deserve to die. The devil whispering that God had abandoned me during this time. Reminding me I was alone and unloved. That even my earthly father did not love me enough to stay. Satan telling me to just grab the gun already aim it at them both and pull the trigger. Giving me the silence that I craved. Again, I asked God, where are you? I could not feel him. In the darkest day of my life, I could not feel God's presence.

I reached for the gun and as they continued to

scream at me, the young teen began to run toward me, I stopped the car. Put it in park and grabbed the gun, I pointed the gun at them both. They stopped in their tracks and looked at me in disbelief. I heard the devil whisper again that they deserved it, just pull the trigger he said. The spiritual battle real as if I were just a puppet on strings and it looked like the devil was going to win this one.

"Stop where you are or there will be more than just my daddy's funeral."

"You can just end it for us here in the street." The lady shouted as her daughter threw something else at the car. I could not make out the words she was screaming. Her daughter throwing things with all her might. Screaming uncontrollably at the top of her lungs. She was almost like a rabid animal; that was out of control.

"Last warning." I called back steadily. As I prepared to shoot should it come necessary to protect my life.

This was someone I knew and her child but, I

knew that my grief was raw and obviously her guilt was raw as well.

Which meant that reasoning with them would not be happening during this time and from the sounds of their raised voices it would not be any time soon.

I watched as the clip slowly fell out of the gun on its own. As I bent to pick it up, I caught sight of the car. As it started rolling down the road slowly, this was impossible I had put it in park.

The car slowly started rolling down the hill, steadily gaining speed. I lost sight of the woman and daughter as I stared at the car. I was sure they were still standing there, but my car.

I watched as the car hit a pothole and jerk toward the ditch. I watched as dad's dog leaped out the open door. Tank ran back to me and stood beside me as we watched the car jump the ditch and hit a tree.

I heard Chenille and her daughter laugh. I heard

them murmur to each other that I was getting what I deserved. I heard them snickering.

I swung back around to face them. I re aimed the gun at the two. Shaking my head, they were not worth the time or energy that I had already spent.

I called for Tank to follow me as I walked to the car.

Chenille and her daughter just stood there and looked at me in utter disbelief and still snickering at the events that had unfolded.

I took a deep breath and thanked God for providing me with enough sense to not kill them in the street. Well maybe it was not sense maybe it was His divine intervention.

Chenille turned with her daughter and walked toward their home. I watched as I thought that this would be the end of it.

Seconds later, I saw them both as they stopped in their tracks. Standing in the middle of the street. I watched as they screamed at me in incoherent words yet again. I knew from experience that this was how they handle things that were beyond their control they felt as if lashing out was the way that gave them control.

It was then that I thought for a moment that I was not any better than them. I was angry and had lashed out too. I knew somehow that this would be the last time either of them lashed out as it would also be mine. Or at least I had hoped.

Through all the chaos I heard God as He yet again told me to leave this to Him. I heard God remind me what I needed to do, I heard God tell me I was not to confront this situation that He would handle what was to come.

I looked at the car, realizing that although an utter mess I could still drive it home. Could this day get any worse? I got in and patted Tank's Head.

I sat in the car with daddy's dog beside me confused and hurting and knowing that this day was only going to get harder with each passing minute.

Hurting for a peace that I was not ready for.

Hurting for answers that may never come.

Hurting for comfort and understanding that would reach depths unknown to those of us on earth.

I was not proud of my choices that I had just made. I was ashamed of my actions. I had failed to remain Christ like.

I begged God to forgive me. This is not who I wanted to become this was not how I wanted to act. This is not how I wanted to be remembered. This was not who I was.

I placed the car back in drive and I drove home slowly. Those three miles seemed like so much many more. My heart still racing from the encounter with my sibling. The guilt of my actions like a wrenching pain in my gut.

I knew I had so much to do but, I did not want to do any of it. School work for the master's classes I was taking. And just all-around general stuff that comes with being a wife, mother, just an adult in general. The thoughts running through my mind that I had to plan a funeral and that.

I did not even know who to call or what to do next consumed my mind. I still had to tell my children. But how? I sat in my car for minutes trying to figure out what to say to the children while they were not babies anymore, they were all teenagers. I looked at Tank as he wagged his tail happily. How would I explain daddy's dog being with me? I let out an exasperated breath. I could not lie; I could not tell them alone.

I glanced at my phone in hopes that Scott was telling me he was headed home. My phone flashed with missed calls from friends and church family as the news spread throughout those who knew me and knew my father.

I had to get into the children before social media told them like it told me. I would not let them hear from anyone else like I did. This is not something that one can prepare their children for I knew that it was going to be hard for them. I also knew that my strength was going to be needed to carry them through the coming days. My face would speak a thousand words without my mouth ever opening. I wanted Scott to hurry home, no I needed Scott to get home I could not tell the children without him standing by me in hopes of avoiding whatever breakdown we would experience from the kids. We had to tell the children before they learned from somewhere else.

I walked into my house. Tank closely behind. The home that I shared with my husband and children. I felt like I was somewhere else, like I did not belong. Not sure what to do or say I decided it was a good time to just clean. We pulled out a kennel for Tank and gave him food and water.

Questions were displaying across my kids' faces. But none of them would ask aloud. It was as if they sensed that now was not the time to ask why we had papa's dog.

Cleaning was my go-to when I could not figure out anything else to do. So, I looked at my girls and told them we had loads of company coming and I needed help getting the house in order quickly. My baby girl looked at me suspiciously but did not say anything. My middle girl went to the sink to busy herself in washing dishes. They had not been home from school long so they could work on their afternoon chores. The usual questions of who was coming over and why were they coming over were being asked however, my face must have delivered the message that now was not the time for questions just to get it done. They began just tidying up the house. We continued until we had the house semi spotless my heart was not in it the house would pass to those just passing through out of respect. I was struggling to keep a positive facial expression. I knew I needed to remain calm and collected until Scott arrived home.

I walked out of the living area and into my bedroom. I checked my phone again. And then I heard my saving grace pulling in the drive. I walked out of my room and headed outside to Scott passing my son as he finally came out of his room. I could not let him see me he seemed to know me better than my girls.

I walked out onto the porch to greet my husband instead of waiting to see my boy. My husband threw his arms around me and pulled me tightly into a hug. I held on for dear life as I was not sure that I could endure breaking my children's hearts with the same news that was breaking mine. He asked if I had told the kids. I let him know that I was waiting for him to get home. Together we walked in the house to face our children. To break their hearts together. I held Scott's hand tightly as we walked to the living room.

I wanted to wait but Scott said now would be easier than explaining why we had waited. That we knew that he would not be coming back the hope of that gone hours ago. He was pronounced dead at the scene there would be no hospital waiting rooms, no miraculous surgery for the doctors to perform daddy was gone and had been for several hours. Several hours before I even knew what was happening as Chenille stood outside and waiting to see how things played out. As dad faced death alone. Tears started clouding my eyes again. I was not sure I could do this.

We called all the kids into the living room. We had to tell the kids before our house started filling with people. Before, I lost control of my emotions. I expected people anytime now as the news was steady broadcasting the incident our privacy felt invaded.

"Kids." I called out across the house.

"Come here for a minute." Scott called to them.

We stood together in the center of the living room. And waited for the kids all to come in. My heart raced as I waited for only a few seconds, but those seconds seemed like forever. I dreaded this.

"Sit down" Scott told them your mother has something to discuss with all of you.

They all sat in random spots across the living room.

I am sure that they thought they were in trouble. Their father had used the serious tone of voice when he told them to sit. I felt like they could hear my heartbeat.

"I have bad news kids;" I watched as they all looked at each other unsure what I would say next. "your papa is dead." I heard them gasp from the information that I just shared. I felt awful because although I wished I could have sugar coated the words for them I knew that there were only so many ways for you to tell them someone they loved was dead. I dreaded the questions that would soon follow. I did not really have answers for them. At least none I wanted to share. I dreaded watching my children hurt even though these babies were not babying anymore they were well on their way to adulthood.

My son would graduate high school soon and was all set to enlist in the service. I knew right then he would not go now. I knew my son well he would talk a big game, but he would be hurting. He loved his papa more than anything and it had not been to long since we stood outside and daddy and he were wrestling. I laughed out loud at the memory of the two skinniest people in the world trying to take each other down. I dreaded to see the pain that would follow. I watched their faces as the realization of the words that I had just said. As the words registered that they would no longer see their papa this side of heaven.

"What happened?" My son asked.

I looked at him and mouthed the words I do not know. I did not have a habit of lying to my kids but, this was not something I was ready to deal with I had not even managed to come to terms with it. Nor was I prepared to answer the questions that would come with it.

"Why?" My youngest asked. To her papa was a hero. He was always great around the kids. And she thought the sun rose and set with her papa. And I would do whatever it took to ensure that this was never taken away from her. She would never know the things in which he was accused.

I looked at her and just shook my head. How do you answer why when you do not understand why yourself and you are the adult?

My middle girl sat in disbelief, tears glassing over her eyes. I knew she was just as heartbroken as the rest even though she tried to appear strong. She was my weak duck. My heart loving baby. She hated when she loses someone to death. Although she was saved and believed in heaven, she hated the thought of never seeing someone again if she was alive. It never mattered what their relationship was or if she only met them once. She was a lover for sure.

"All I know is he killed himself. And now we wait and see what details follow. And what information they find as they investigate his death."

I knew the rest of the story. However, I also knew that my children would be protected for as long as I could keep the news out of the house. It would not be long but, maybe I could shield them for a short time from the details that surrounded his death. I was not sure, and I did not know what to do or say when it came to the detail questions of why, how, or any other question. The details that would haunt me for the next several days. They were just learning that life was unfair. And that the devil works harder when you are one with God. Only a couple hours in and Satan was hard and strong on top of me.

They nodded their head as if to just accept the news of losing their grandfather. The saddest part was watching the grief play across their faces was knowing that I could do nothing to take away their pain.

I felt the same pain that was on their faces, I was feeling the same emptiness, the abandonment, the confusion, the multitude of emotions playing at its own pace within each of us. Acceptance would not come for many of us. And somewhere across the world acceptance would never come.

Friends arrived with hugs and kind words that were meant to comfort. But nothing soothed the hurt we all felt. With pasted smiles across our tear stained faces we faced the world with our heads held high and our hearts broken.

As the afternoon turned to evening the crime scene was almost completely processed. It would not be long before I would have to go back to dad's and face the crime scene. At least the Sheriff said that they would call me later. I guess I really had to wait and see. Some sweet soul fed the teenagers. While I sat and just wondered how I was going to carry on. I had already planned to take off work and had called to explain the situation to the boss. I thought this was the process that I was supposed to follow. I knew that I would not get much sleep as the afternoon turned to evening and my mind continued to race. I dreaded the moment that I would have to walk through the house that belonged to daddy and see the evidence that he would no longer be coming home. I was not ready. I was not ready to say goodbye.

When that call finally arrived armed with my husband and close friend, I left the children with each other and family friends and Scott and I drove to dad's house we were greeted by several officers and the sheriff. Scott of course wanted to know why I had to find out from the news. And in Scott's ever loving straight forward tone he asked. Why? Of course, that appeared to get his attention. Scott just might get some answers. I have never seen him act of this nature. I was not sure if it was emotions from dad's death or if it is from seeing me break down. I was always the strong one in our relationship. But this no one was prepared for.

Seven

∽

Chapter 7

I often wondered what was going through the Sheriff's mind as my husband and friend quizzed him on his process. As the Sheriff answered their questions and looked at me for assurance. I knew that we were just dancing around the elephant in the room. Nothing mattered now. My father was gone and no words nothing would make him come back. I asked right then could I see dad's body. My husband looked shocked. My friend told me no without waiting for the sheriff's answer. I repeated the question. I want to see my father's body; Can I see it? My tone harder than I initially intended.

"Sheriff, I want to see his body? I want to see what he did to himself." I stated again. I was annoyed that no one was listening to what I wanted.

"Ma'am, I am sorry the corner has already taken

the body to the morgue and in the morning, he will leave for the GBI crime lab."

"The crime lab?" I looked confused I was not understanding any of this.

"Yes, your father was taken to the crime lab for an autopsy. It is normal procedure for these types of situations. Now, I need to prepare you for what you are about to walk into to."

Scott looked at the Sheriff and said what we were all thinking, "What do you mean what she is walking into?"

"Well, when your father opened the door, he came to the door with a pistol in his hand. He stated that he had nothing to say to us and shut and locked the door back. Standard procedure is to back away from the situation. We called to him several times over the intercom he never answered us. Then we heard the gun shot. Not knowing if anyone else was in the house with him we shot tear gas into the home. Now the door has been opened however it is still strong inside the house. Now It is my recommendation ma'am that you let someone else go inside and you remain out her with us. As there is still some evidence of what has transpired here today in the house and I am not so sure you want that memory:"

I looked at the officer with a straight unemotional face and asked him exactly what he meant to define evidence of what has transpired. What exactly was he not wanting me to see?

"There is still a pool of blood by the front door." The sheriff looked at me expecting me to agree instead what he got was a strong-willed daughter.

"Sherriff, thank you for the warning but I will be going inside the house. I can go alone if needed. But I am going inside. I got this."

The sheriff looked concerned as the other officers stood nearby. I took a deep breath and walked to the front door. I had to appear strong. I had to appear together, or Scott would pull me out of here. I walked inside with my head up. The tear gas was strong. I walked inside and looked in dads' room, it lay empty without a sign of life. I walked into the kitchen and living room and sat down on the loveseat that my father had sat on earlier that day.

The tears streamed down my face as I looked at the congealed blood that lay by the front door. The blood almost appeared as if it was fake something pulled out of the movies to make it look real. I sat staring at it as if picturing my father lying beside it.

I wanted to know how they found his body lying. I wanted to see those pictures. I wanted to look at what he was wearing when he came to the door. I had to know I wanted to see I looked around and no one was there. No one I could ask those questions too. I stared at the spot in the floor the spot that showed that this was not a dream. The spot that would forever be etched into my mind. The details were uncanny. It was safe to say that I would never forget the way the blood was pooled or the shape in which it stopped running. I just wanted to know why. Why end things like this?

"Daddy, why?" I let the tears fall as I heard the voices of my husband and friend. I had not even realized that I had spoken my thoughts out loud. I wonder if they heard me, I could hear that they were talking about the tear gas that I was exposing myself too. Little did they know I was numb and could not even tell it was in the room.

"Karlyn, are you alright?" Kate asked.

"Yeah, I am alright."

I looked up at Scott who was standing beside me.

"What do you want me to use to clean this up?"

I looked at Scott as if he were speaking another language. He pointed to the blood by the door. As if he was directing me back to this time and place. A place that I was suddenly forced back into. I felt like I was out of my body completely. I knew that the trauma of what I was seeing was the cause of this feeling. I also knew that I was not alone. I knew I had my amazing husband beside me but, I felt a stronger presence, a stronger sense of peace that I could not possibly put into words.

"I do not care honestly. I guess a towel is fine. Whatever can you find really?"

"There's only white towels."

"Scott, it's fine I promise white, black, whatever is here. I'm not washing it we will just throw it out."

Scott grabbed the towel and bent to wipe up the blood. I watched as he spread the towel over the spot and used his hands to bring in each side to wipe it away.

I felt the tears pour down my face as I struggled to catch my breath in the house filled with tear gas. I could not wipe my face with my hands, or my shirt, or even the paper towels across the room. My face burned; my eyes burned. The tears continued to silently fall as I watched my precious husband do what no family should have to do. I did not understand why the sheriff's office left this for the family to clean up. I would be sure to ask though. Just not today?

"Honey, Are you okay?"

I was not sure if I was crying because of dad or because my amazing husband was cleaning up my father's mess, he left behind.

"Yeah."

I continued to watch as he cleaned away the last of my father. The blood had already congealed as the sun hit the floor of the living room. I cried a little harder as Scott finished the cleaning and stood up.

Together we walked out of the living room and into dad's bedroom. We gathered all the valuable items and anything else that looked as if I was supposed to pick it up. Papers from his computer desk, his fireproof safe, and the rifles he kept put up. With each trip to my car to load the few things the harder it was becoming for me to keep it together. I was more concerned with people breaking in and stealing the things they could pawn who knew when I would be able to handle coming back inside and dealing with his belongings.

As we screwed the doors shut, I said goodbye to dad again, one last time.

I knew he was already gone.

I knew that he could not hear me.

I knew it was silly to think that saying goodbye at his house would make me feel better. And for a short time, it really did. I knew by night fall left alone with my thoughts the tears would come and would come hard. I was not ready for night fall, but nightfall was coming quick. I felt like I could make it through this but, as the minutes passed, I was not sure if I would ever be alright again.

Scott drove us home and him and Kate walked inside I opened the trunk to look through dad's things. I could feel the tear gas on me. Kate was going home to shower quickly before anyone touched her. We were advised to use cold water to rinse off before using anything else. I walked inside and rinsed off and traded my clothes for the non-tear gassed ones. I headed back out to the car and grabbed a notebook that I had taken from his computer desk. I thumbed through it just seeing bill payments and passwords, important items but nothing that stuck out as to the questions that I had on my mind. I had not gotten extremely far when it opened to an envelope with my name on it.

It was in that split second that I lost all the control that I was pretending to have over my emotions and tears. Kate came out of the house to see me laying on the concrete parking pad the letter clutched in my hand tears streaming down my face as I cried for my father. She held me as I cried into her arms. I could not even finish reading the letter dad had left me.

My eyes were clouded with tears I could not even breathe. Parts of me wanted to die in that instant. I knew that I was not enough to keep my father alive. He had written his final words to me only three days after I had asked him was committing suicide on his agenda of dealing with the things that he was going through. Then in that time and place he had said no, however today spoke another story and his final words to me was written and I could not even answer back. I could never tell him how unfair all of this was.

Dear Karlyn,
Take care of Tank for me.
Handle my things as you see fit.
Pin number to the card is 8155.
Land Payment is paid it is due on the 13th,
Titles are all signed to you for the house and car.
Do not, I repeat do not do anything for her.
She is dead to me.
Karlyn, I will haunt you if you do. It is all yours.
Dad.

There was no I love you, there was no words of redemption, no admission of guilt. Absolutely no information that I sought. Nothing that would tell me the answer to the question that was taking over my mind. Why? There was just handle things and for me to take care of Tank. Handle things meant that I had to rely on God to walk me through my next actions. Because I had already shown myself that blood was not thicker than water when it came to family. How was I supposed to handle things when I could not even stand to look at her? How was I supposed to forgive and forget when I really wanted to aim and shoot? I was angry, I was furious, I was heartbroken. And no one seemed to understand that I was not just one emotion I was many different emotions all at the same time. The real question was How was I supposed to accept this and plan a funeral when I was not ready to deal with any of this? And take care of Tank, Dad you were supposed to do that. It is why I gave him to you. I did not want another dog I already have six.

I continued to cry into Kate's arms; I watched as Kate passed the letter over to Scott. Who read it and said we would get through this? He was not understanding that I really did not want to get through this I just wanted it all to go away as quickly as it appeared. His words of encouragement filled with special meaning and love for me, landed on empty ears tonight. His usual soothing voice annoyed me as he spoke kind words. He did not get it. I mean how could he. His parents were alive and well.

I just wanted a time machine to take me back to days when things were easier, when I could talk to dad, when dad was here, and I could change his mind before he did something of this caliber. The final decision he would ever make on this earth was a decision that I could do nothing about and a decision that would change my life forever.

I walked inside with the letter in my hand. The family and friends eventually went home. Truth was I almost wished they had all stayed. Because now it was the biggest test. Could I go to sleep without dreaming of his death? My mind was racing with thoughts of different scenarios. With thoughts of what could have been. With thoughts of how I should have been there. Thoughts of the things I should have said. This was all my fault; I did not save him. I did not deserve to live. I deserved to die too.

That night proved to be the hardest as I cried myself to sleep. I could only sleep for a few hours before I was awake again and again crying. The cycle continued until morning. I felt awful my husband did not get much sleep and even though his hugs were sweet, and his embrace secure nothing was going to make me feel any better. I had lost my father the day before. To a scenario that I had only ever read about. I had no idea how people left behind from a loved one's suicide survived this. I knew that I could not function like this. I knew that I had to do something I just was not sure what to do. I also knew that somehow someway I had to come to terms with things.

Eight

∿

Chapter 8

Chapter 8

I pulled myself together enough to get dressed and make myself look presentable. I had things to handle, and I could not sit here all day wishing I too, were dead. I walked out of the room only to find my youngest was sitting there waiting on me.

"Shouldn't you be at school?" I asked.

"No ma'am I am on babysitting mom duty." She replied with a smirk.

"You are kidding right?" I looked at her in disbelief.

Her father would not have put this child on babysitting duty would he.

"No ma'am daddy said to stick by you like glue."

Of course, he would. And that sounded just like what Scott would have told her to do. He had no choice but to go to work today. Even though I know he did not get much sleep last night. I could do this though I did not need a sitter. I left the house with my teenage babysitter in tow. We went and arranged most of dad's funeral service. I turned the life insurance policy over to the funeral home to handle.

I ordered the funeral flowers and picked an urn. I choose to have him cremated which was his wishes when he passed away. He had told us this for years. I could only hope that my sister would agree as she had to sign off on it as well. The funeral home guy was amazing as he laid out my options and ensured me, he would handle getting my sister to sign. I could not pick a date for any of this until the body was returned from the GBI lab. I was not sure how long that process would be. I had planned just to take a few days off handle the funeral etc. But life always seems to throw curve balls when I least expect it, and this would be a huge one.

The returning of the body proved to be full of struggles and trials that I was unprepared for. I had so many decisions to make that I was not sure if I was coming or going. I walked over to the flower shop and just stood in the flower shop, I could not make my mind up on flowers all I knew was that I was supposed to order flowers and while I did not know exactly what to order for a cremation service or even when this service would take place, I had to do something. Eventually I just left and went home.

I was not accomplishing anything, and I figured I could just google some pictures and send over to the florist. Obviously, I had time to look at whatever my heart desired as I had no idea when his body would be released. With every flower picture my heart turned heavy, and tears streamed from my eyes. A parent gone to soon.

Some say it never is easy when you lose a parent.

That losing a parent is extremely hard it is something you can never prepare for. I believe though watching a parent become sick and continue to decline must give you some type of peace as at least you have the chance to say goodbye even when it is the last thing you want to do. I can tell you when you lose a parent to suicide the feelings are tremendously unbearable. You do not have that moment of goodbye; you do not watch their health decline or have that chance to wish they no longer were suffering. You talk to them one day and the next they are gone before your eyes as you watch the news blast across your cellphone screen before anyone contacts you from the scene. And you instantly wonder why you or the grandchildren was not ever enough of a reason to live before they make the final decision to take their lives. It is a question without an answer. A learning of how unfair life will seem.

The hours turned to days and the week began to pass. Dad's body still had not been returned. Life really seemed to just stop but at the same time life carried on around me as if I was an unwilling participant. Every day was a struggle just to get through. Praying for the hurt and pain to go away. Praying to just get things over with. Each prayer bringing you closer to Jesus's feet because this situation had broken you in ways that you never dreamed possible.

You are really seeking a comfort that your spouse, children, siblings well honestly no one here on earth can really seem to provide you. In a moment of frustration, wishing for answers and comfort. I opened the Bible, I tried to read some of it every day a chapter, a verse or sometimes even two. But nothing seemed to be helping. I was hurting in ways that I had never hurt before. It was an ache that nothing seemed to ease. No words of comfort from friends, no words of comfort from family, nothing was easing the ache that seemed to go so deep that only a miracle would heal.

I knew that this was an internal conflict with my faith and my doubt of how God could allow this to happen. I wanted to scream at God. I was angry in ways that I could not put into words. I was not sure that God was even listening to me anymore. As I read the Book of John over again nothing seemed to stick out. I kept reading and continued to find myself at the same verse repeatedly. As if I was committing it to memory. Instead, maybe this is what God was trying to tell me that in him I would find the peace that I was seeking.

"I have told you these things, so that in me you may have peace. In this world you will have trouble. But take heart! I have overcome the world."
– John 16:33

What God do you think you have told me? I

screamed at God. Because you did not tell me he was going to die that day. You sent me to work. I could have stopped him God. I could have saved him. The tears were hot against my cheeks as the wind softly blew against my face. Sitting by the pool in the blazing sun looking out over the trees I watched as the limbs did not move and the wind blew softly across my face. A peace that I was seeking and had yet to find, found itself upon me. Now silent I listened.

"I have told you these things, so that in me you may have peace. In this world you will have trouble. But take heart! I have overcome the world."

– John 16:33

You did not tell me God. You knew and did not prepare me. Shouldn't you have warned me? I mean do not you send angels or something to warn us of things? I mean you sent Mary an angel! How could you say that you love a person like me when you did not prepare me for this? Aren't I your child? Do not you love me always? I do not understand God. I do not get it. I just do not understand, and I really want to do that God I want to understand.

Greeted by silence and a gentle breeze the breeze strong enough to turn the pages of my Bible. This would be usual on a breezy day, but the wind seemed silent as I looked out into the field of open trees. Looking down the pages were still turning and then pages stopped turning, I looked down to find the Bible turned to Jeremiah. The first verse I read at the top of the page.

"For I know the plans I have for you," declares the Lord, "plans to prosper you and not to harm you, plans to give you hope and a future."
– Jeremiah 29:11

God, I do not understand what you are trying to tell me. You had to remove my father from my life to help me prosper, for my future, for hope. Sounds like an excuse God. This is not why my father died. What is your real excuse was he already terminally ill? Is that what you do not want me to know? I was obviously still bitter and angry as if a couple of hours talking to God would miraculously cure the anguish I felt after just a couple of days of dad being gone.

I sat silent for a few moments allowing God to explain how I would prosper and His plans for me. I did not understand why it seemed dad had to be gone for me to prosper I did not understand how making me uncomfortable would change anything in my life or even in my sister's life. Because truth have known her life would be more affected by his death than I would ever be. She depended on dad more than I ever did. I called just to talk about random stuff. Tank the topic of our conversations most days. I read the two verses again and closed my Bible.

"Oh God I know you are there, and I am sorry I am angry, I do not know what I am supposed to feel. I want answers, I want revenge, I want things to go back to the way they were just days ago. Just wake me God from this awful dream. And Lord if you are not going to wake me from this dream, if you are not going to give me my father back, then Lord could you please just carry me through this. Just carry me." I felt the tears slide down my face as my prayer fell from my lips.

I replayed the verses again in my head. Trying to

get a clue for what God had planned. I knew my life was going to change. This much I knew already; it already had. But I was not sure how God thought it was going to change so dramatically. What was His plans for me exactly? And how did removing my only parent have anything to do with the plans God had for me? Yes, my mother was still alive, but truth being told daddy dying had me less likely to rekindle a relationship with my mother than anything else. I was beyond tired of trying with the woman that birthed me. I genuinely believed that there was a mental disorder lying in her brain that she refused to seek help on. I was finished being the ugly duckling daughter. I wanted God to show me my true potential, I wanted to serve Him wholly and fully. I wanted Him to have the glory for everything I did from this point forward. I was not sure how to ensure that I did that but, I knew that this was something that I was going to make sure happened.

Nine

~~

Chapter 9

Two weeks Later

It has been two weeks since dad died. I still do not see any changes around me. Things seem impossibly worse than ever. Dad's brothers coming out expecting a handout. Claiming to have proof that they were to have this and yet never proving anything. Lucky for them I believed in being fair. Unlucky for them I do not scare easy, and I stand my ground. After all I was my father's child, I did not run from anything I always went after what scared me the most. And usually, I always got what I set my sights on. His body had just come back from the lab and I requested to see his body before they sent him for cremation. I was denied in the gentlest manner that one could be denied for a request of this magnitude.

"Karlyn, you do not want the last memory of your father to be this. He has been gone for over two weeks Ms. Karlyn. It just is not a good sight. His body is decomposing. He is hardly even recognizable. I cannot let you do this on behalf of husbands everywhere if you were my wife, I would not want you to see your father like this."

"Sir, I just need something. I need to see that it was really him. I need some closure. You must understand. I hear you guys tell me my father is dead. I see the pool of blood at his front door as it sat congealed. However, I still need to see his body. I need the closure."

"Karlyn, let us just send you a couple of pictures after we get him cleaned up. Can you live with that?

That way you see that yes, it is really him. And it will give you the closure that you need yet, save you from seeing his body. Ms. Karlyn it is just something that would never leave your mind. And you could look at the pictures whenever you feel like you can handle it."

I knew I was running out of options it was clear that I was not going to be allowed to visually see him. So, I agreed to this compromise. I was driving when the picture text came through. I wanted to pull over right away and look at them. But I knew that I did not need to do that. I was not so sure I could handle wait awaited on that screen. I was scared but, knew that this was the only way that I could have the closure that a part of me sought. I could not really put into words what I was feeling. There were so many emotions running through me at once. I pulled into my driveway and looked down at my phone again. I parked in the garage and grabbed my phone.

I opened the text message and there was the picture that I had begged for. The picture for the closure that I sought so desperately. I looked at my father's face, the purple tone of his skin, the bruising from the trauma that he had experienced to his body. I looked at his mouth that held the smirky grin that he was so known for it was shining brightly from my father's face as if he was laughing at me from the grave.

Knowing that I could not stop him from doing what he had decided. I could not change his final decision.

Oh, Daddy, why? I asked the picture as if it

would answer me. I knew this was where I was supposed to cry, and I waited for the tears that never seemed to come. I begged my eyes to water, to tear up; to do something. Nothing came, no tears, no screams, just silence as I stared at my father's picture with his eyes closed for the final time and his lips curved in a smirk. That was my memory of my father. I could not remember another time of what he looked like. I saved the pictures and locked my phone. I never locked my phone but until those pictures were not the first ones you have seen on my phone; I knew that I had no choice to protect my children in case they decided to open the pictures or text message when they happened to look at my phone.

I continued to feel like I was drowning, my emotions on overdrive. I was not sure how I could make the decisions that needed to be made. To make decisions that would be fair and treat my sister equal when I wanted to do the complete opposite. I knew that I was still overwhelmed with grief and I felt alone. I did not know anyone that knew this pain. And being alone is not a great feeling to have. This is when I it did not matter how many people stood in front of me offering their support. I needed something more it was not filling the huge hole this experience was leaving in my heart. This incident was leaving me with more questions than answers and more decisions than I really wanted to make.

I did not know what I needed to do. He was officially at the funeral home and it was time to decide the funeral arrangements. I went to the funeral home and suffered through borrowing an urn for the funeral as dad was to be cremated before the service. I had placed the order for the flowers and picked a time. The church was to feed the family, preacher was covered. Songs were picked. What seemed like should take forever to plan was done in less than an hour. I could only hope that this would be what daddy would have wanted. But the hardest part was not knowing for sure where daddy would spend eternity. And this was the hardest part of his death. Of course, I had taken the time and prayed with dad. It had been recently. We had discussed God and salvation, heaven and hell. But in my mind the question lingered was he a saved by Faith man or was dad headed to hell to spend eternity. Nothing could change his decision it was too late for that.

How many other people have I allowed to die without being saved that I could have witnessed to?

How many others had crossed my path unsaved that I had let walk This was the question that was haunting me more than why he decided to take his own life? I could not fully explain the details of the questions that lingered did I say enough to him to ensure that if he was not saved as a child that he was saved as an adult. Did he know that Jesus died for him too even though he was not ever at church that all he needed was to believe and repent? Was believing and repenting enough? Did I send my father to hell because I did not say enough or did not say the right things? Would I ever know?

Day and night this haunted me. And no one on this earth could answer the question that I found myself asking repeatedly.

I found myself crying for the lost soul that I was scared that I had caused to go to hell because I was too scared to share my faith. Was my broken heart a part of the overall picture? Was I supposed to be this broken so I would turn to God more? I felt like screaming at God in ways that I probably should not, but I wanted answers. I deserved answers. But was I prepared for the answers that God would show me?

Ten

～

Chapter 10

Ever feel like God is playing jokes on you as if God has a sense of humor? Some of the things he gives us to go through at times is hilarious stuff.

Especially when you see the outcome. I talked with Chenille and we agreed that once the death certificate arrived, I would just handle everything.

The paperwork was filed his assets handled. His bills paid that could be paid with what money there was. Loans taken over to avoid losing the property that our father cherished. Life seemed to smooth out finally.

The house was gutted and remodeled to remove all signs of tear gas and the death that had taken place. A new beginning for it. I was starting to heal.

Chenille was finally pulling her life together. I knew it was hard for her. But I also knew that whatever God had in store for us it was going to take the both of us to overcome together what we had been through. I swallowed my mountain size pride and started being there for her. We sat and talked for hours. Spent time together. Started being the siblings that we both longed for and forgot how to be over the years. For once we sat united.

Sitting during my quite time I asked God was this what He had in mind. Was this why my father had to die? You see I still blamed God. It had been weeks but, nothing had changed for me and yet everything had changed. No one knew what to say to me. No one knew rather to hug me or just walk by. I did not know what I wanted or where I wanted to go. I just wanted the pain to go away. His death still felt as fresh as the day he died. A nightmare that I was not sure I would ever wake up from. I still did not have any more answers than I had right after his death. I opened the Bible and just thumbed through it. I knew somewhere in this Bible that I loved to read when times were rough, and I loved to read the history of and how we articulated the Bible into sixty-six books. Theology was something I loved. I remembered talking with Dad about the Theology course I took and how we discussed so many things that the theologists debated on. The Bible found itself to John. The shortest verse it seems in the Bible that I could recall anyway. John 11:35 "Jesus wept." God are you telling me that when I cry for my father you cried too? I surely did not understand this verse. I could not make the connection with what I was struggling with and how Jesus' weeping had anything to do with it. Sure, Jesus cried while on earth I mean the man was ridiculed because few believed who He really was. He was separated from His Father, to die for our sins. Of course, Jesus wept. But to think that Jesus wept because I wept was impossible or was it?

In frustration I shut the Bible. I was not getting anywhere. I opened my phone to social media and there at the top of the page was a message that appeared to have been created for just me and my time of distress.

"Faith Begins at the End of Your Comfort Zone."

God what do you mean that faith begins at the end of my comfort zone. None of this makes me comfortable. I just want my life to go back to the way it was three weeks ago. You know when I was just living my life to the fullest and serving you in church, trying to figure out other ways to serve you.

Doing homeland missions with the orphans in group homes. Loving on foster children every chance I got. Interacting with people I did not know for a cause that was dear to me.

Why did you have to take my father God? Could not the bullet have missed anything vital? WHY LORD WHY? I shouted.

I wanted God to help me out here, show me what it is that you want me to do so bad that you had to take me out of my comfort zone. Just show me the reason that daddy could not stay. Show me the way that you want me to go.

I knew God was not going to answer me right away.

I knew that I was going to have to pray this same prayer for days, weeks, maybe even months before God felt it was time to reveal to me what I was supposed to do. I tried to carry on as usual until it was time to say our final goodbyes. I went to work, I cooked dinner, I attempted to socialize but inside I was losing who I was, and I was not sure that I liked the fact that this Karlyn was going to be accepted by those who I loved the most.

Twenty-one days after his death dad's funeral was held.

As if this day cannot get any worse. The time has come to say our goodbyes. The urn is placed, the flowers are centered. The funeral home is ready to go. The songs are picked out. We sit and wait for family to show up. And no one shows. Only people to support me. I see Chenille walk in with her children and with another couple. Maybe everyone is just running late. As the time continued to pass, I realized that this would be a small group. That dad's so-called friends were not showing up; that his brothers would remain long lost. I get it that suicide is hard. I get that circumstances are not ideal. I get that one would not want to be tainted with the memory. However, what happened to the meaning of family. I realized that no one seemed to remember that families were supposed to stick together. I realized that siblings drift apart. I realized that one's way of life would influence their decisions to attend with others that may not have the same belief that they have.

The service started the songs were played; the preacher started preaching. He tried to encourage those of us left behind. As he knew that I personally was having the hardest time with this. He attempted to share where we would spend eternity without knowing Jesus Christ as our Savior. He admitted to not having the opportunity to personally meet my father. But he admitted that he had the privilege to know me. Some made the comments that dad was not religious, and they did not understand why we had a preacher to talk about God. The reality of it is the funeral service is not for the deceased the funeral service is for those whom the deceased has left behind. The service ended quickly; I felt empty. I felt lost. There were a few tears shed by his grandchildren. I personally was having a hard time showing my emotions in public. I knew that once I left the funeral home the tears would eventually flow. However, I knew being in public meant personal appearance was to hold everything together. No tears to cry, no emotions, one was to remain pulled together. I am not sure where that came from but, it was the way it had always been for me.

We left for the church that had prepared way too much food for the people that attended the funeral. I was embarrassed that no one showed for his funeral service. I was embarrassed for the things people were saying. I was embarrassed for the situation all together. I did not know how to overcome something of this standing. I was not so sure I ever would. Statistics show that when a parent commits suicide the children are more likely to commit suicide as well. Would everyone always wonder if I was contemplating suicide?

Little did I know God had huge plans and this was only the start of those plans. I was officially out of my comfort zone. The familiar people gone from my life. The reason that I never talked of my past gone, saved from embarrassment of any words I had to say.

The calling from God was something that I could no longer ignore. Sleepless nights, dreams of large stages, dreams of people from all walks of life, pictures of future me on stage. Life was about to get interesting, and the people God would choose to put in my path were people that I would have never thought of myself interacting with.

If anything came of this event it is the reality that family is important. This itself made me realize that I was going to change my own way of life. I was going to start spending more time with my family.

Those that were blood and those that were not but might as well be. I planned to make time for not only my children, but my extended family, my church family. I was going to change the way I treated everyone and check on everyone instead of waiting for them to check on me. I was going to make myself more available for different things instead of immediately saying no. I was not sure where to start exactly but, felt God would lead me into that direction.

Days after the funeral life was still a list of unanswered questions. God was still showing up and showing out. I was still learning what my calling meant. I was being asked to speak more than ever before. Something that I did not ever dream of doing. I was speaking out against suicide. I was offering suicide prevention training. I was speaking out for foster care regulations to be changed. I was no longer being quite for the things that I believed in. You cannot make a difference if you choose to stay on the sidelines. And God had chosen me to stand among the crowds to make a difference in many things. And making a change was what I planned to do.

Eleven

∽

Chapter 11

A Year later

Life was moving along steadily. It had taken six months to get dads death certificate so that I could apply to handle his estate affairs. That was finally done and what was able to be paid was paid or whatever needed to be done.

I still found myself talking to Tank and telling him that dad would be by to grab him soon. Tank boy he is not coming to get you he is gone. As I whispered that to Tank, I thought to myself you and I buddy must accept that.

Cardinals were everywhere. The deepest red color you could imagine. I would find myself talking to them though as if daddy would talk with me through them.

I could not understand why dad did it. I could not understand what dad was thinking. Most of all I could not figure out if dad were guilty or not. I knew his past, but did the past define the present. I would never know. Regardless of the information that I knew. The truth of the matter was it no longer mattered. He was gone and knowing the details would only hurt more.

Life goes on after death. The good, the bad, the ugly. You carry on and adjust your life around those that are no longer here. Never forgetting them just learning to live without them. Wanting to call and yet knowing that they will not answer.

Life after death. Trying to make life the same again. With every passing day. People say time heals all things. And it does not heal all things.

After dad's death I thought I was really alright. However, the thoughts started trickling in. The thoughts of how life would be for my husband and my loving children. After all they did not need me. I was not worthy of my husband's love. I was useless. Just working to pay the bills I created. Buying things daily as if I had an unlimited supply of money.

The emotions continued to trickle in. The hopelessness of never being good enough. The despair of never looking good enough. The harder I tried the worse my performance as a spectacular wife and mom became. Friendships died. My oldest best friend abandoned me when I needed her the most. Who was I kidding? I did not have real friends.

Friends that stay. If I were honest my friends were only the ones that I could help at the time. It appeared that if one could get money from me, they were there my best friends. Or the friends that needed a babysitter, Or the friends that needed you during a trying time in their life and then when all is well you too are out in the wind.

A real friend that would support me for whatever, whenever. That was what I needed.

So many changes were taking place inside my heart and mind. Things that I had trouble wrapping my mind around. I was tired of how life was. I loved my little family that I created. Husband, kids, animals. But I needed an outlet. Something that I could just be me on. I just wanted a place to release and not have judgement.

I could teach dance exercise classes, maybe even a step class. That would be perfect for me. I signed up for the classes, learned all the moves. A lady gave me a chance and after training she released me into my own little class. I lasted for less than four weeks and she fired me.

Wait What? I had never really been fired before this was a first for me. I thought I would be crushed, I was not. I felt relief from having to stick to a schedule on certain nights. Me with no schedule. Not a chance.

Who was I becoming?

What happened to the Karlyn everyone knew and loved?

I was unsure myself. The Karlyn everyone loved always said yes, never argued, was kind and soft spoken, always with a pleasant smile upon her face.

Life had begun to harden me. All the pain, disappointments were starting to take its toll upon my body and even my disposition. I had always heard that your environment changed you. I did not believe it until I began to live that out.

Twelve

∽

Chapter 12

Chapter 12

The realization that I had become hard was hard to swallow. Is this why I did not have friends. I mean

I had friends that I spoke to on the phone and via text message.

I knew something was wrong I just could not put my finger on it. It was going on the second anniversary of my father's death. And I had slowly tried to move past the past and try to give mom another chance. I was calling almost weekly. She seemed to talk as if she had her stuff together. But if we are being honest there was this deep dark hole that I was trying to climb out of and talking to her made me slip further down instead of helping me out.

Twenty-three months after my father's death I started completely losing sight on reality. With every breath I took I no longer wanted to breath. With every breath I took, I dreamed of car crashes where I would be sure to die.

It was with every breath I took; I knew that my family was better off without me.

Who had I become?

Where had I lost myself at?

Real Christians Real lovers of Jesus do not think of committing suicide?

Jesus protecting them, right?

I was seeing a new side to what the world new as

suicide. I was seeing and feeling utter hopelessness. All while putting on a fake smile.

Scott was annoyed. He was remaining pissed at Karlyn. He had no idea what she was going through. Maybe she was seeing someone else. She had withdrawn so much these last six months. She did not want to go anywhere or do anything. She never brushed her hair or even fixed her makeup anymore. Scott knew things had been difficult the loss of her dad and sickness with him and his parents. Life the last twenty-three months had taken its toll on all of us. But Scott was fine. The kids had adjusted. So, what was wrong with her?

The last phone call had Scott so pissed off with Karlyn that it was finally the straw that broke the camel's back as the older generation said.

"Karlyn, I do not know what the heck is wrong with you but get out of this funk you are in. Or get the hell out of my house! And you can take your extra baggage with you. I do not know who he is but, if he is all you can consider thinking about you can do it on your dime not mine."

"Who he is? What are you talking about?"

"Karlyn, just stop with the dumb act already. I know you are seeing someone. I know that is why you stopped dressing to ensure I looked at you. Why you stopped telling me you love me? I watched you for months now and your actions tell me we are done? That you have moved on to someone else. And I will too. I will find someone grateful for what I provide her with. That loves me for me.

It was a slap in the face to my already brittle soul. I had withdrawn so much that he had no idea I was completely lost. I read the Bible every day. I prayed every day. But there were no friends to reach out to for help. I was utterly and completely alone. And if Scott thought I was seeing someone that would add even more to my already depressed state. I loved Scott with everything I had. Even on the days when he was an agonistic butthole. He was still my butt-hole and I loved him.

I tried a brave face. I tried a fake smile. I tried to aim my car for the river, Dang auto correct. I prayed harder, I read more of the Bible, I lost myself in everything that I thought would help me. And nothing helped. I was destined to die at my own hand.

And my husband had no idea.

Thirteen

~

Chapter 13

My Choice

I got into the car on Saturday morning I was tired. Scott was gone to an auction. The kids had their own lives to live. I petted the dog's bye. Even feed them treats at the door. Little did they know that this would be the last time that they see me.

I looked at the house one last time as I drove out of the gate and watched it close. I felt a tear stream down my face as I said goodbye.

I stared down at my purse, the letter to my husband sticking up. The letters to my kids sitting with stamps ready to be mailed.

It was Saturday and Saturdays meant no traffic no one to interrupt. I turned out onto the usually busy street. I drove for several minutes before turning onto a deserted dirt road. I turned into the unused driveway of a field and looked out into the clearing. I could see the family of deer running through the far end of the field playing. I could hear the squirrels and birds playing in the trees.

I looked down at the letters, I looked at my phone. No one had missed me. And they would not miss me when I was gone.

I had written all the passwords down. Added

Scott to every account I had alone. It was pure ridiculous really. I had given Scott access to anything I was not sure he had access too.

I was done.

This was my end.

It was time I ended my misery.

And made my love ones happy again.

They would be so much happier if I were not around.

There was no sense in them suffering if I could take it all away.

I looked up into the clear blue sky.

"God take me home, to Jesus's arms."

With those words I leaned back into the seat and waited for the pills to take me away.

Fourteen

~

Chapter 14

I felt cold. I could hear beeping in the distance. Heaven was awful cold.

I thought it would be pretty and warm wonderful flowers blooming. I could not smell them all I could smell was the powerful aroma of uhm was that alcohol. And what was steady beeping. I did not recall reading anywhere in my Bible that there would be an obnoxious beeping in heaven.

I really needed to send a message to the preacher so he could tell the others about this obnoxious beeping. And the smell.

Oh and why could I not see. Why were things black?

I wanted to check everything out.

I had watched enough shows to know that when I got to heaven my family that had gone before me would greet me. Where were they?

Where was grammy, and dad? My little friend Megan and her mom Carol.

Oh no, was I doomed then. Did I fail at my faith?

The only thing that was greeting me was a chill and a steady beep.

Oh no what if God was punishing me for taking my own life. What if he was sending me to hell instead?

The beeping increased. I could hear talking but could not make out the words. I could feel pressure on my hands. A burning sensation going through my arm. I tried to move my mouth and open my eyes to see but the blackness took me away again.

Fifteen

∽

Chapter 15

While you were sleeping.

"Doctor, will she wake up?"

"Scott, I do not know. Medically speaking there is absolutely no reason that she should not wake up. You are basically waiting on her."

"You mean it is up to Karlyn if she wakes up?"

"Yes Scott, we have done all we can do. It is up to your wife from here on. Her brain is functioning, her heart is working properly. Medically she is fit. But something spiritually is holding her, keeping her from waking up. The only thing left to do is pray. In the meantime, Scott, we need to talk about long term."

"Long term, what do you mean."

"Scott, we need this room. This bed for other patients. You are going to have to look for a long-term facility for her or take her home."

"I can't take her home like this. What am I supposed to do with her?"

"It isn't a decision you have to make today. Get her kids here. You guys talk things out and come to a decision that all of you can live with. In the meantime, maybe just maybe, God will hear your prayers and she will wake up."

The doctor took another look at Karlyn and with that he nodded his head and walked out the door. Holding on to her hand was not enough for me. I craved her. And I do not mean sexually. I craved her laugh as I slapped her butt as she walked by. I craved her laugh that she did as she walked by and slapped me back. The way her face would light up when I wrapped my arms around her. The way at night fall she climbed into my lap and wrapped her arms around my neck and give me a kiss on the cheek and neck. I took those moments for granite. I would give anything to hear her snore one more time.

I missed my wife.

I crawled next to her in the bed. I am sure it was a sight to be seen after all I was over six foot tall and every bit of two hundred and twenty pounds. But I had to get close to her. I had to let her know I wanted her here. I was not ready to let her go.

I snuggled next to her; I could smell the faint scent of her dry shampoo still lingering in her hair.

I had brushed it just this morning lightly using dry shampoo so that she would still look like herself if she would just wake up.

I began to whisper my thoughts to her in her ear. Tears flowed from my eyes.

"Karlyn, honey listen to me please just wake up. I do not know why you thought I could ever live without you but, I cannot. Just open your eyes. Baby, what about the kids? We can get you some help. We can do anything that you want! Just come back to us. Just come back."

I laid my head beside hers as tears streaked down my face. I could not stop them. If there was ever any doubt about me loving my wife. It should be gone now.

I loved my wife.

I thought about all the jewelry that I bought was enough to show her just that. I thought all the things that I purchased her would show her just how much she meant to me.

In honestly it did not, as Karlyn was trying to kill herself. She must not know that I could not live without her.

"Oh, my precious Karlyn."

I would never forget that phone call. The phone call that told me that my precious wife was being treated for intentional harm. She had to wake up she just had to.

"Lord, I know that you are not use to hearing from me. I know Karlyn is the one that does all the praying for us. But Lord I love you too. I do. Please do not make me sacrifice my Karlyn to show you just how much I love you. I know that I cannot bargain my way with you to get you to answer my prayers in the way that I want them answered. Bring my wife back to me. Let her wake up."

Sixteen

❧

Chapter 16

I opened my eyes to find Scott lying next to me. I felt smothered as his arm was draped over my check. He was clutching my hair in his hand.

I tried to raise up only to realize that I could not lift my head. It seemed like it weighed a hundred pounds.

Scott opened his eyes.

He smiled; a smile so big it reached his eyes. I could not remember the last time that he smiled that big at me.

"Karlyn, your awake?"

"well yeah."

"Honey I am so glad that your awake. I love you so much. I will be the best husband ever from this day forward. Please please do not leave me prematurely again."

He kissed my head. My cheeks, and slowly ever so lightly on the lips.

"I love you to Scott, and I am so sorry."

The nurses walked in and seen Karlyn awake they called for doctors.

The whole floor came walking into the room.

Surprised yet so happy to see her awake.

I watched as Scott slipped out to call everyone and tell them that I was awake.

I was scared for what everyone would say. My life, my choices, my bad decisions. Would I ever get past this?

Church members poured in, flowers, were everywhere. Why did everyone wait for something drastic to happen before they showed you, they cared?

The next voice caught me off guard.
It was the voice of my sister.
Why is she here; I thought to myself.

"Well Karlyn, how's it going?"

"Chenille, I am doing fine. Why are you here?"

"Karlyn, your my sister regardless of hateful words, or even actions at the end of the day we are sisters."

I looked at Chenille in disbelief. This was not the Chennille that I knew. It was unbelievable. Was this the reason that I could not go and die and live-in heaven forever. Was it so my sister and I could forgive each other?

I hugged her back as she hugged me. It felt good to have my sister by my side again. After what we had been through we really needed each other. We would never agree. Our lifestyles were different. But, then again maybe somewhere down the way our lifestyles really were the same.

"Karyln, I have to go to work now. I love you. Get better and no more crazy stuff okay."

I watched as Chennille walked out the door.

I did not do this for attention.

I watched Scott, walk into the room. He smiled that genuine smile. I smiled back and motioned for him to come here.

He walked to the each of the bed and bent and

kissed me lightly on the lips. I had missed him so much. Missed this.

"Scott, Do you forgive me?"

"Honey, forgive me. I had no idea that you were suffering like this."

I watched as a tear fell from his eye. I watched as it rolled down his face and I knew that we would make it through this.

Seventeen

∾

Chapter 17

A Second Chance

I was a struggling writer with my newly published books among the best sellers in the local bookstore. Okay so who was I kidding. I was not even in the bookstores.

My books were only online to order as an on-demand print. I had not sold two copies while the famous authors sold out almost daily. I wanted to promote. I really did.

But I feared being in front of the camera. I was really scared that I would find myself amid a pity party for the connection of my father. I was scared that people knew that I had tried to end my life as well. I did not want a pity party or a walking on eggshell friendship. I was done with the "oh, poor Karlyn, her father committed suicide and she failed at committing suicide."

I knew that I just could not handle that lady like.

Let us face it there was a lot of things that I could not handle lady like. But at least I was forgiven. I think. I am fairly sure God forgives me for being reckless some days.

I sent emails out to the Governor's Office regarding changes to the foster care system that so desperately needed to be made especially to their adoption system. Someone would eventually listen. It was not fair to hold someone else's choices against you and I wanted to make a difference.

I knew that my suicide attempt was not going to help me give a child a home. I knew that it showed that I was mentally unstable. If they would just let me adopt. Things would be different. I wanted to give a child a home, I wanted them to feel loved. But I was not so sure that adopting was what I was supposed to do. But I knew a change was coming. I knew that my God given calling was speaking out against foster care and in some way my father's suicide ties into this.

I had conducted an interview with a local podcast out of the governor's hometown regarding my books and foster care. It was something of a passion lately that I could not seem to put to bed. Everyday this passion seemed to grow bigger than the day before. I was slowly starting to realize what God meant when he said, "Faith begins at the end of my comfort zone."

There were a couple of things I knew for certain my faith was stronger since my father's untimely death. Not to mention my lost 2 weeks when I attempted to follow in dad's footsteps.

God and I seemed to talk more about things than ever.

I was reading the Bible more intensely than I ever had. I knew what a mustard seed looked like and realized that my faith had grew bigger than the tiny mustard seed I had always pictured.

Armed and ready for whatever God had planned I started reaching out to different resources to get on the governor's schedule. And when his office called to schedule the appointment you would have thought I had won the lottery.

October 23rd is the first time that I received a call from the governor's office requesting my presence for a meeting on changing the foster care regulations. He wanted to hear what I had to say. He wanted to attempt to put a different stance on the foster care system in our state. His office claimed that talking to a former foster child and someone who had the opportunity to interact with other former foster children and the current ones that I could offer insight.

The following week could not come fast enough. I was packed and ready for my three-hour drive to discuss these issues with him in his office in Savannah, Georgia. I was nervous but this topic gave me passion that no one could seem to understand.

And the reality was that God was right I would have never called the governor's office with my father alive. I would have never stepped out on faith until the last year had unfolded.

I had grown out of my shell in ways that I never dreamed was possible. I had grown so much in not only my faith but, in so many other ways as well that I knew what the verse meant when God said he equipped the called. Well, that was not His exact words that he gave to us in

Luke 11:9-13

"So, I say to you: Ask and it will be given to you: seek and you will find; knock and the door will be opened for you. For everyone who asks receives; he who seeks finds; and to him who knocks the door will be opened. "Which of you fathers, if your sons ask for a fish, will give him a snake instead? Or if he asks for an egg will give him a scorpion? If you then, though you are evil, know how to give good gifts to your children, how much more will your Father in heaven give the Holy Spirit to those who ask him!"

I had asked for a big change. I had asked for direction. I had asked to make a difference. And in turn God was answering in ways that was surprising everyone around me.

Oh, and did I mention that I was now hated by my biological mother for this same change that God was creating within me. What else was new though anything that made her children better than she had become was immediately of the world and not of God.

I had flown across the United States to stand among many wanting to bring suicide awareness to the foster care population. Many foster children commit suicide this was a reality that I, myself, had not even realized.

However, what floored me the most was learning that my father, was a part of foster care as well. My dad a foster child but back then it was a bit different he was raised by family, so he did not get that title. But it sure made you wonder if the history contributed to the depressive state that led to his suicide. It was a study that I planned to ensure was completed in my lifetime to ensure that the number of suicides especially among our foster care children was reduced and possibly eliminated.

I also knew that if we could reduce the suicide numbers down completely among all age groups and previous history it was something that I wanted to be a part of. I was not sure how or what to say but

I knew that without a shadow of a doubt that God would give me the words to speak when the time came to address the issue.

I knew that we would never know for sure why my father decided he could not face tomorrow. But I also knew who held the answers. And when the time was right God would show me what I needed to know and understand and until then I was okay living a changed life. A life that I now gave ultimately and unconditionally to Christ.

Eighteen

~

Reader

Dear Reader,

Thank you for choosing to purchase this book. I hope that you enjoy the words that are portrayed here. I pray that if suicide has touched your life from losing a loved one or from considering it yourself, I pray that you find comfort in knowing you are not alone.

I want to take a moment and talk about the loneliness that one must feel to contemplate suicide. I know that you may possibly feel like there is not another way out but whatever the circumstances are surrounding your choice I pray that you seek out a trusted friend, pastor, or even a suicide counselor and talk about your feelings and circumstances and ask for help. And if you want to reach out to me, my information is at the back of this book. I will personally respond if you are thinking about committing suicide and reach out to me for help.

If you are that person striving to move on from losing a loved one and currently blaming yourself for not seeing the signs. It is not your fault. The signs were probably there, things that you never thought about pointing to your loved one's feelings. These things are out of our control. As much as you blame yourself for not seeing the obvious signs, they were not meant for us to see my dear friend. I never thought my father would commit suicide until fifteen days before he did. And friend I just knew without a shadow of a doubt how things were going to turn out. I even asked my father, and his answer was of course I am not planning to commit suicide. But, fifteen days later he was dead from a gunshot wound to the head. Does being right make me feel any better? Not a chance. Did I blame myself? Yes, I did and some days I still do. I blamed myself for days and weeks and even today I find myself thinking I should have done something. I should have removed the guns from the home. I should have reached out to someone on his behalf for help. Instead, I did nothing. I believed him; I trusted the words that he spoke. And friend it is okay to trust that person and the words that they say. Because in the end there is not anything you can do to prevent what they have set into place. Some would disagree with that statement and maybe you feel like you could stop it. If it makes you feel better, I believed that to until I could not stop it. My friend, that blames themselves, I see you hurting, and it is okay my dear friend you are not alone in your pain. I feel your pain too, I understand that you feel like it is your fault, and I know that you want answers to why and answers to what you could have done differently. I have these thoughts almost daily and while we may never know why, know that there is nothing that you could have done differently to change the outcome.

After my father's suicide I reached out to several groups for training for prevention of suicide. I learned the signs, the cues to know what they are thinking. I sought information after information. In an endless search for answers. The sad part is armed with all this information will not bring my father back. Armed with this information and looking back will not change his decision. And even looking back at the weeks or months before his death the signs that he showed of thinking about suicide were not the obvious signs that I learned from QRP Training.

However, my newfound friend. While we struggle to find answers to the cause of them feeling hopeless. While we look back and see the signs that we blame ourselves for ignoring and not seeing then. While we make scenarios up in our head of things we should have said or done; I hope that I can convince you to instead sit and pray because God can help heal that feeling of guilt. It is a burden that we never should carry alone.

And my friend, know that no time will heal this wound. You will have days that you dearly miss your loved one, you will have days that you cry and ask yourself all over again why. Know that it is okay. It is okay to miss your loved one, it is okay to admit that you do not understand, and it is okay to even be angry with them for taking matters into their own hands. But my friend holds your head up and continue fighting for your dreams do not get lost in your sorrow or grief because you matter too. Allow God to use this trial in your life to help others that maybe close to you considering this decision or have lost a love one to suicide.

May God use this book for healing of the broken hearted. May he heal you in ways that are not explainable. May you see your self-worth and understand that suicide is not the answer to your life's problems. I love each of you. And pray that you see how much God loves you.

Nineteen

༄

Afterthought

I debated how to end this book. I cannot say that dad's Final Decision did not change my life. I cannot say that I think about him every day or that I pick the phone up to call him. What I can say though is that God's grace carried me through those rough days. I still have a long way to go to be healed completely if that is even possible here on earth.

As we go through the Covid-19 pandemic I thank God for dad not being here to suffer through this mess. With his bad health he would have gotten the virus and I still would have been unable to say my goodbyes.

Reader, I also want you to know that if you are the person that is contemplating suicide and feel as if you have nowhere to turn please visit my authors website and reach out to me. Let me help you through these thoughts and put you in contact with the most loving assistance you will ever find. Jesus Christ. You are loved, you are enough.

Reader, if you are struggling moving on because a loved one has committed suicide. I want you too to reach out to my author's website I will help you just as God has helped me through the same thing. I promise you will not be turned away. We have people that can help you overcome this depression. Kalaholton.com

Suicide is not easy, and it contributed to me trying to assist others in no longer being homeless or jobless.

The hardest thing is that in a couple of years you will start to see the hopeless feeling that your loved one carried. It will become almost more than you can handle. As I sit here on the other side of that hopeless feeling, I want you to know that there is a reason for tomorrow. I want you to know that those that love you really do love you.

Love Your Sister in Christ
Kala Holton